For Mitch, Ken, David, and even Debbie —S.L.
For Wilma and Hannelore —M.L.

Text copyright © 2020 by Suzanne Lang
Jacket art and interior illustrations copyright © 2020 by Max Lang

All rights reserved. Published in the United States by Random House Children's Books,
a division of Penguin Random House LLC, New York.

Random House and the colophon are registered trademarks of Penguin Random House LLC.

Visit us on the Web! rhcbooks.com

Educators and librarians, for a variety of teaching tools, visit us at RHTeachersLibrarians.com

Library of Congress Cataloging-in-Publication Data
Names: Lang, Suzanne, author. | Lang, Max, illustrator.
Title: Grumpy Monkey up all night / by Suzanne Lang ; illustrated by Max Lang.
Description: New York : Random House Children's Books, 2020. | Audience: Ages 3-7. |
Audience: Grades K-1. | Summary: "Jim Panzee goes to a sleepover where he wants to stay up all
night long to do fun activities. But one by one his friends fall asleep. How long will Jim be able to
stay awake?"—Provided by publisher.
Identifiers: LCCN 2019036275 (print) | LCCN 2019036276 (ebook) |
ISBN 978-0-593-11976-1 (library binding) | ISBN 978-0-593-11975-4 (hardcover) |
ISBN 978-0-593-11977-8 (ebook)
Subjects: CYAC: Sleepovers—Fiction. | Chimpanzees—Fiction.
Classification: LCC PZ7.1.L3437 Gu 2020 (print) | LCC PZ7.1.L3437 (ebook) |
DDC [E]—dc23

MANUFACTURED IN CHINA
10 9 8 7 6 5 4 3
First Edition

Random House Children's Books supports the First Amendment and celebrates the right to read.

GRUMPY MONKEY
UP ALL NIGHT

By Suzanne Lang

Illustrated by Max Lang

Random House 🏠 New York

Early in the evening—just about suppertime—Norman heard
a whole lot of whooping and hollering next door.

"What's the ruckus?" Norman asked his neighbor Jim Panzee.

"I'm so excited!" Jim exclaimed. "I'm going to a sleepover at my parents' house!"

"My whole family will be there! Mom, Dad, and my big sisters, Ann and Nan!"

"Who's that?" asked Norman.

"Oh yeah. My little brother, Tim," grumbled Jim.
"But never mind. It'll still be fun."
"Sleepovers are a good time," Norman agreed.

Jim talked about all the great
things he would do.

"First we'll go termite fishing."

"Next we'll tell scary stories."

"Then we'll have a midnight feast."

"And wash it down
with some jungle punch."

"I wouldn't drink punch too close to bedtime," Norman advised.

"Bedtime?!" exclaimed Jim. "Nobody sleeps at a sleepover! We're going to stay up all night!"

"Sounds fun," said Norman. "Mind if I tag along?"

A little later, they arrived at the tree where Jim's parents lived.

"It's my little Grumpy Monkey!" Jim's mom cried as she gave him a hug. "I'm so happy to see you!"

"Mom!" moaned Jim. "I'm NOT little! And I'm not a monkey! I'm an ape!"

Jim's mom smiled and ruffled his fur. "But you sure are grumpy!" she said.

"No, I'm not!" Jim scowled.

"I like your mom," said Norman.

"No fair! You didn't say we could bring a friend!" said a voice coming down the path.

"Who's that?" asked Norman.

"Tim!" exclaimed Jim's family.

"I thought you said he was your *little* brother," said Norman.

"I had a growth spurt," said Tim.

"What should we do first?" asked Jim's mom.

Everyone answered at once.

"Termite fishing!"

"Pick fleas off each other!"

"Bob for mangoes!"

"I know," said Tim. "Measure each other to see who's tallest!"

"Maybe our guest should choose," suggested Jim's dad, turning to Norman.

"It's a tough decision," said Norman. "It all sounds fun."

"Don't worry," said Ann. "There'll be plenty of time to do everything because we're going to stay—"

"UP ALL NIGHT!" cheered Jim and his siblings.

"I don't know," said Jim's mom. "Staying up all night could make for some very grumpy monkeys."

And then the games began.

TERMITE FISHING

FLEA PICKING

BOBBING FOR
MANGOES

"It was a dark and stormy night," said Jim.
Tim trembled.

"Your brother's scared," said
Jim's mom. "Why not tell a happy
story instead?"

"It's really dark," said
Tim, looking around.
"Because it's night,"
snapped Jim.

"Are you grumpy?" asked Tim.

"No!" said Jim.

Just then they heard a noise.

RAAAAA

"Thunder!" shouted Tim, and his eyes went wide. "Oh no, now it's dark *and* stormy."

"Don't worry," said Jim. "It's just Norman snoring. He does lots of funny snores. Sometimes it sounds like *raa-raa-raa-raa*, and sometimes it sounds like *prfffffprfffffprfffff*." Tim laughed. "Other times it's like *haaaaWEEEEEhaaaaWEEEEE*!"

Jim and Tim laughed and laughed all night long.

As the sun came up, Tim fell asleep.
"Good idea, little brother," said Jim as he
tucked Tim in and lay down.

But just as he was about
to close his eyes . . .

"Good morning, my monkeys!" sang Jim's mom.

"Mom!" shouted Jim. "We're not monkeys! We're apes!"

"I prefer 'gorilla,' but yeah, 'ape' works," said Norman.

"Oh, Jim, I told you staying up all night would make you grumpy," said Jim's mom, ruffling his fur.

"I'M NOT—"

"You'll always be my Grumpy Monkey,"
whispered Jim's mom.